Tips for Reading Together

Children learn best when reading is fun.

- Talk about the title and the pictures on the cover.
- Look through the pictures together and discuss what you think the story might be about.
- Read the story together, pointing to the words and inviting your child to join in.
- Give lots of praise as your child reads with you, and help them when necessary.
- Have fun finding the hidden mouse.
- Enjoy re-reading the story and encourage your child to say the repeated phrases with you.

Children enjoy reading stories again and again.
This helps to build their confidence.

Have fun!

Find the mouse hidden in every picture.

The Monster Hunt

Written by Cynthia Rider
Illustrated by Alex Brychta

OXFORD
UNIVERSITY PRESS

Gran took the children on
a monster hunt.

Biff saw some monster
footprints.

Chip saw a monster glove,
and . . .

Kipper saw the monster!

"Come on," said Gran.
"Let's get that monster!"

The monster ran.

It ran up the hill.

It ran into the mill . . .
and hid.

"Come on," said Chip.
"Let's get that monster!"

They went into the mill.

"Ssh!" said Gran.

"I can see the monster's tail."

Gran pulled the monster's tail.
"Got you!" she said.

"AARGH!" said the monster.

Crash! went a sack.

Crash! went the monster.

The monster looked at
the children.
"Help!" he said.

"Monsters!"

Think about the story

Why do you think Gran and the children went on a monster hunt?

How did the children know which way the monster had gone?

How would you feel if you got covered in flour?

Would you like to go on a monster hunt? What would you do if you caught the monster?

Matching

Match the monster to its shadow.

More books for you to enjoy

Level 1: Getting Ready

Level 2: Starting to Read

Level 3: Becoming a Reader

Level 4: Building Confidence

Level 5: Reading with Confidence

OXFORD
UNIVERSITY PRESS

Great Clarendon Street,
Oxford OX2 6DP

Text © Cynthia Rider 2006
Illustrations © Alex Brychta 2006

First published 2006
All rights reserved

Series Editors: Kate Ruttle,
Annemarie Young

British Library Cataloguing
in Publication Data available

ISBN–13: 978-019-279230-3

10 9 8 7 6 5 4 3

Printed in China by Imago

Have more fun with Read at Home